This book belongs to.

. . . .

. . . .

Retold by Monica Hughes
Illustrated by Priscilla Lamont

Reading consultants: Betty Root and Monica Hughes

Marks and Spencer p.l.c.
PO Box 3339
Chester, CH99 9QS

shop online
www.marksandspencer.com

ISBN 978-1-84461-813-2
Printed in China

First Readers

Read Together

The Princess and the Pea

MARKS &
SPENCER

Helping your child to read

First Readers are closely linked to the National Curriculum. Their vocabulary has been carefully selected from the word lists recommended by the National Literacy Strategy.

Read the story

Read the story
to your child
a few times.

The prince opened the door and there stood a girl.
"I am a princess," said the girl.
The girl was beautiful and wore a crown.
But she was very wet!
The prince liked the girl. But the queen said, "I will see if she is a real princess."

16

Follow your finger

Run your finger under
the text as you read.
Your child will soon begin to
follow the words with you.

Look at the pictures

Talk about the pictures. They will help your child to understand the story.

"I am a princess."

17

Have a go

Let your child have a go at reading the large type on each right-hand page. It repeats a line from the story.

Join in

When your child is ready, encourage them to join in with the main story text. Shared reading is the first step to reading alone.

Once upon a time there was a lonely prince.

"You would not be lonely if you got married," said the queen.

But the prince didn't want to marry just anyone.

"I want to marry a princess," he said.

"I want to marry a princess."

The next day he went to look for
a princess.
He saw beautiful girls.
He saw girls who wore crowns.
But they were not real princesses.

He went to look for a princess.

The prince went back to see the queen.
He told her about the beautiful girls
and the girls who wore crowns.
He told the queen that they were not
real princesses.

The prince could not find a princess to
marry.
So he was still lonely.

12

The prince could not find
a princess.

That night there was a big storm.
There was thunder and lightning.
Then it rained and rained and rained.

In the middle of the night there was a
knock at the door.

There was a big storm.

The prince opened the door and there
stood a girl.
"I am a princess," said the girl.
The girl was beautiful and wore
a crown.
But she was very wet!
The prince liked the
girl. But the queen
said, "I will see if
she is a real
princess."

"I am a princess."

So the queen got a hard dried pea.
She made a bed for the princess.
The queen put a pea under the
mattress.
She put twenty mattresses on the bed.
She put twenty quilts on the bed.

The queen put a pea
under the mattress.

"This is your bed," the queen said to the princess.

The princess had never seen a bed with twenty mattresses and twenty quilts.

The princess climbed into bed.

"Good night," she said to the queen.

The princess climbed into bed.

But the princess could not sleep.
She was awake all night.

In the morning the queen came to see
the princess.
"Did you sleep well?" asked the queen.
"No, I was awake all night," said the
princess. "There was something hard in
the bed."

The princess could not sleep.

The queen went to see the prince.
"She is a real princess," said the queen.
"She felt the pea under twenty
mattresses and twenty quilts.
Only a real princess could do that."

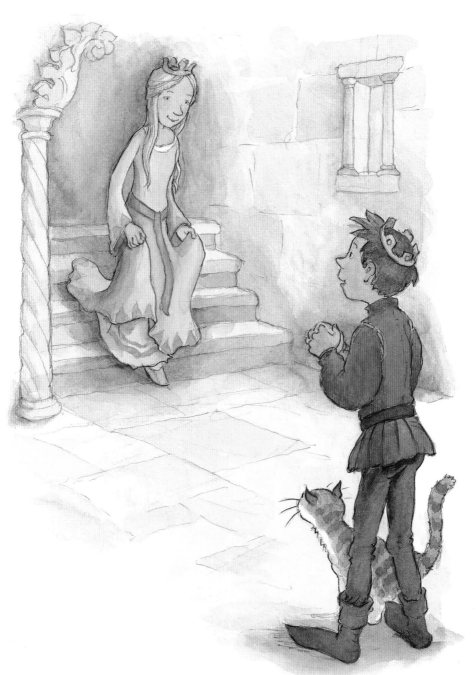

"She is a real princess."

At last the prince had found a real
princess.

"Will you marry me?" he asked.

"Yes!" said the princess.

They were married the next day.

The prince was never lonely again and
they all lived happily ever after.

They were married
the next day.

Look back in your book.
Can you read these words?

prince

peas

queen

mattress

princess

Can you answer these questions?

Who came to the
door in the middle of
the storm?

What did the
queen put under
the mattress?

Who did the
prince marry?

Read Together

Look out for other books in the **First Readers** range (subject to availability):

Fairytale Readers